W9-CLX-370

Disney's STORYTIME TREASURES LIBRARY

Now the magic of Disney's beloved animated films comes to life in these eighteen all-new stories. Read about favorite characters such as Aladdin, Belle, Snow White, and Simba, Timon, and Pumbaa in tales that communicate gentle messages from which every child can benefit. While children delight in brand-new adventures filled with humor, adventure, and fun, they'll also learn about cooperation, respect for others, learning from mistakes, good manners, and many other valuable tools for life. A poem at each book's end ties both story and message together in a delightful rhyme children will love to recite and remember.

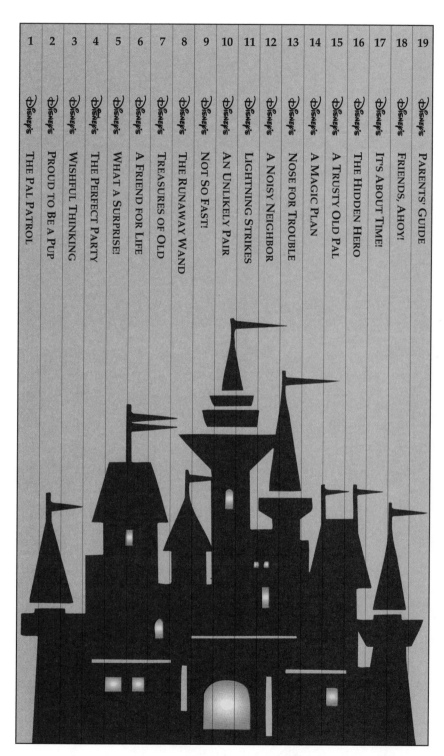

The books on the spines are numbered and titled:

1. Disney's THE PAL PATROL
2. Disney's PROUD TO BE A PUP
3. Disney's WISHFUL THINKING
4. Disney's THE PERFECT PARTY
5. Disney's WHAT A SURPRISE!
6. Disney's A FRIEND FOR LIFE
7. Disney's TREASURES OF OLD
8. Disney's THE RUNAWAY WAND
9. Disney's NOT SO FAST!
10. Disney's AN UNLIKELY PAIR
11. Disney's LIGHTNING STRIKES
12. Disney's A NOISY NEIGHBOR
13. Disney's NOSE FOR TROUBLE
14. Disney's A MAGIC PLAN
15. Disney's A TRUSTY OLD PAL
16. Disney's THE HIDDEN HERO
17. Disney's IT'S ABOUT TIME!
18. Disney's FRIENDS, AHOY!
19. Disney's PARENTS' GUIDE

Collect all the books in Disney's Storytime Treasures Library and create a keepsake library of all-new stories your child will enjoy for years to come!

Published by Advance Publishers
© 1998 Disney Enterprises, Inc.
All rights reserved. Printed in the United States.
No part of this book may be reproduced or copied in any form
without the written permission of the copyright owner.

Written by Jamie Simons and Nancy Casolaro
Cover illustration by Peter Emslie and Edwards Art
Design and editorial illustration by Vickey Bolling
Produced by Bumpy Slide Books

ISBN: 1-57973-015-9

10 9 8 7 6 5 4 3 2

Disney's STORYTIME TREASURES LIBRARY

PARENTS' GUIDE

Beautiful princesses. Good fairies. Lovable talking animals. Castles. Far-off lands. Stories filled with these and other magical images will prepare a child for a lifetime of reading enjoyment. Now Disney's Storytime Treasures Library brings this enchanting world of reading right into your home.

Research shows that the most important thing that you, as a parent, can do to help your child become a reader is to read aloud to him or her. Reading opens new worlds to your child and stimulates the imagination. The closeness of sharing a book together can set up the association of books with good feelings. Experts agree that when reading is fun, your child is on the road to success.

When you read to a child, he or she is excited by the prospect of learning to read. There are several things you can do to help prepare your child to read:

- Be an example. Have books, magazines, and newspapers around. Let your child see you read. When reading is a part of daily activities, a child thinks of reading as something that everyone does. It becomes an activity in which he or she wants to share. Consider having a family reading time. You can read a book or newspaper, and your child can "read" a picture book, the comics, or a magazine.

- Read to your child regularly. Spending some time together every day is the key. Even fifteen minutes at bedtime will be a reading memory your child will cherish. As your child grows and begins to read, ask him or her to read to you sometimes, too.

- Make sure there are plenty of reading materials around the house. An inexpensive way to have a variety of books is to use your public library. As soon as your youngster is old enough (usually when a child can write his or her name), get him or her a library card. Until then, use yours to explore this rich world of learning. While you are at the library, take advantage of the storytime programs for your child. Many libraries have a story hour, show films based on books, or have visiting storytellers.

- Encourage your reader. Have your child tell you a story. When you read to your child, ask him or her to turn the pages. This will help reinforce the idea of reading from left to right. Discuss the pictures. Often these are powerful clues for what is happening in the story. Remember, you are your child's first and most important teacher! The goal here is to instill in your child a love of reading and to make your youngster a lifelong reader.

- Help develop your child's listening and speaking skills. An important part of reading is language development. A child needs to have heard words before he or she can read them. Talk to your child. Go for walks and outings and talk about what you see. Encourage dress-up play, creating a wonderful opportunity for your child to use imagination and to make up dialogue.

- Provide opportunities for your child to hear different sounds. Have him or her listen to the sounds animals make, to everyday inside and outside sounds, to rhyming sounds, and eventually to the sounds of letters.

- Help your child be aware of the words in his or her immediate environment. Point out the words on cereal boxes and street signs; play guess the brand logo or store name. Let your youngster see that words are useful.

How to Use This Guide

This guide was developed by educators and tested by children. For each book in the series, there is a section that contains a short summary of the story. This is followed by questions designed to increase your child's understanding of the story and to help develop his or her comprehension skills. Then there are the activities. Have fun with the hands-on projects, crafts, recipes, and games with your child. Make reading come alive!

Getting Started

Provide pencils, markers, crayons, paper, and child-safe scissors. Keep these tools in a special place where your child can always find them. As you read, encourage your child to draw pictures about the story. Look at an illustration in the book. Ask your child to draw what came before this picture, and what happened next.

When you read the stories aloud to your child, try occasionally pointing to the words. This will help your child make the association of letters on a page with spoken words.

If your child enjoys it, play some simple sound games. Read a sentence and listen for the words that begin with "b," like "Bambi." Look around the house for objects that begin with "b." Have a "b" picnic of bananas and bread and butter.

Most important of all, enjoy! Reading is one of the great pleasures in life. Let Disney's Storytime Treasures Library help you and your child pave the way to enjoy it all the more!

Disney's
THE
LION KING

THE PAL PATROL

Timon gave his pal a playful tap. "Oh, well," said Timon. "At least we don't have any responsibilities to tie us down. Let's go have some fun. Whaddaya say?"
"I say, 'hakuna matata,'" Pumbaa replied.

"Exactly!" agreed Timon.
And so the two wandered off into the brush, looking for grubs — and whatever adventure might come their way.

Since becoming the Lion King, Simba has no time for taking life easy. His friends Timon and Pumbaa do their best to drag him away from his responsibilities, but duty calls. Determined to have a fun and carefree "hakuna matata" day, the pair go looking for grubs. Instead they find a wildfire, and Timon rushes off to get help while Pumbaa warns other animals to stay away. The two are heroes after Timon returns with a herd of elephants to put out the flames. Simba appoints them the Pride Lands' official fire patrol. This tale teaches that:

- 🐾 work well done is a source of pride.
- 🐾 accepting responsibility feels good when something important can be accomplished.
- 🐾 it is important to balance work and play.

Put On Your Thinking Cap

Read the story through to your child once. After she has experienced the whole story, allow her to display her own "mastery" of reading. Here are examples of simple questions that will help your child recall

what happened:
- Why is Zazu upset with Pumbaa and Timon?
- What do Pumbaa and Timon like to eat?
- Who does Pumbaa warn to stay away from the fire?
- How is the fire put out?

The most basic comprehension skill is simply recalling what has been read. A more advanced step is to question "why." Use these "why" questions to get your child's imagination going:

- Why do you think Pumbaa is named Pumbaa?
- Why do you think Timon is called Timon?
- Why do you think neither of them likes to work?
- Why do you think they like to eat insects?
- Why do you think you don't eat insects for dinner?

Stop, Drop, and Roll

This story is a good jumping-off place for some basic fire safety lessons. Points you might want to cover:

- The dangers of playing with matches.
- The family safety plan. Discuss how your child can escape from her room if there is a fire. Tell her where everyone should meet outside the house if you're separated. Does your child know not to hide in case of a fire?
- Press the smoke alarm button so your child knows what it is, what it sounds like, and what to do if she hears it.
- Explain to your child how to "Stop, Drop, and Roll."
- Make sure your child knows how to use the phone to call 911 in case of an emergency (calls should be made from a neighbor's in the case of a fire).

Lions
(and Timons and Pumbaas — oh, my!)

Help your child create her own stand-up Simba and Pumbaa figures.

Fold a piece of construction paper in half.

Cut out the legs, as shown. Then cut a slot across the front and back. Use another piece of paper to draw and cut out a head and tail.

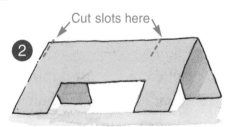

Cut slots here

Push these into the slots. Finish by having your child color the animal and paste yarn or paper bits for whiskers and tail tip.

Walt Disney's
101 DALMATIANS

PROUD TO BE A PUP

Missy, wanting to join in the fun, said, "Did I help, too?"

"You just watched, the way you always do," said Freckles. "Anyway, you're too quiet to help. You can't even bark!"

It was true. Missy had never barked — not once in her whole life. "I could if I wanted to," she said in a soft voice.

"Really?" said Freckles. "Then show us."

The Dalmatian puppies act out scenes where they triumph over Cruella De Vil. Shy little Missy, one of the puppies, is left out of all the fun because she can't bark. Missy decides she'll become a cat and takes lessons from Sergeant Tibs, the brave cat who helped rescue the puppies from Cruella. Missy does not make a very good cat, and all her efforts end in failure. But when a couple of crooks try to steal the pups, Missy, in desperation, barks a warning. The robbers are scared off, and Missy is a hero. From then on Missy is happy to be a Dalmatian. Missy's story teaches children that:

- happiness comes from being yourself.
- everyone has useful skills.
- you can go to your friends for help.
- people like friends who are quiet and thoughtful just as much as they like those who are outgoing.

Put On Your Thinking Cap

The most basic comprehension skill in reading is remembering what happened. Assist your child's recall by asking simple questions:

- What story do the puppies love to act out?
- Why does everyone laugh at Missy?
- Who helps Missy with her cat lessons?

- When does Missy finally begin barking?
- How does Missy feel at the end of the story?

Everyone has times when he wishes he could be just like someone else. This story provides a great springboard for role playing. Here are a few questions to help tie together the story and your child's imagination, while at the same time encouraging him to recall what happened in the story:
- Why does Missy want to become a cat?
- What animal would you choose to be?
- Can your animal make a sound that would scare others away?
- If you could be anybody or anything in the world, who or what would you be?

Guess Who

Roger was able to guess that Missy was trying to be a cat simply from the ways she acted. Children and adults can have a lot of fun playing at being different animals. While one of you takes a turn acting like an animal, the other guesses which one you are. Older children may enjoy creating and answering simple riddles like this: "I am very small. I like to eat cheese. Cats chase me. I make a squeaky sound. Who am I?"

Acting Up

The puppies dressed up and acted out their own play. Encourage your child to put on a play for you. A dress-up bin of old Halloween costumes, Mom's fancy dresses, Dad's old hats, and any uniforms lying around are a never-ending source of childhood amusement. Don't forget to include some props: play phones, toy cash register, paper plates and cups, and dolls. A really elaborate production could involve drawing scenery and making pretend tickets to "sell" to the audience. Older

siblings can get in on the act, too. If your child is having trouble getting started, have him pick out a favorite book and act out the story. Or have your child try acting out these more familiar scenes:
- Your pet rat gets loose in the house.
- Today is the day of your birthday party and the guests are beginning to arrive.
- Your older brother takes away your favorite toy.
- You go to a friend's house to play and your friend won't share her toys.
- You are a parent and you are shopping at the mall with your child.
- Your family goes to dinner at a restaurant.

It's Great to Be Me!

Missy learns that it's great just to be herself. Help build your child's self-esteem with this activity. Spread a long sheet of newsprint or butcher paper on the ground. Have your child lie on the paper while you trace his outline. Let your child decorate his paper "body" using yarn for hair and old fabric scraps for clothes. Hang the finished product on his bedroom door.

1. KINDNESS
2. CHARITY
3. GIVING

After Jafar had finished, the Genie turned into a schoolteacher and asked, "What have we learned today, Jafar?"

"That if you're as rotten as I am, goodie-goodies like you can make life a misery! Now make your third wish already!"
"Oh, dear," said the Genie, pretending to be upset. "I think you need an attitude adjustment!"

Jasmine and Aladdin enter the Cave of Wonders, where they find a magic lamp. They bring the lamp back to the palace, where their friend, the Genie, rubs it. Out pops the evil wizard Jafar, and he is very, very angry. Unfortunately for Jafar — but luckily for the world — the Genie is now Jafar's master. Believing that even mean old Jafar can do something positive, the Genie orders Jafar to do only good deeds. Thoroughly upset at having to be so kind, Jafar is finally returned to his lamp. Children can learn from this story that:

- exploring can lead to unexpected adventures.
- good deeds are their own reward.
- being kind is always a good way to act toward others.

Put On Your Thinking Cap

Young children are excited by the idea of learning to read. It is a great mystery that they want to master. You can help make reading more familiar by reading this story, then asking simple comprehension questions like these:

- What was creating such a disturbance in the Cave of Wonders?

- Who was inside the magic lamp?
- What good deeds was Jafar forced to do?

A powerful comprehension skill is to try to understand a story from the viewpoint of one of the characters. Go over the story again with your child, asking her to pretend she is Abu the monkey. As you go through the story again, ask questions like these:

- What is Abu thinking in this picture?
- If he could talk, what would Abu say now?
- What does Abu think will happen next?

Cave Cookies

These delicious cave cookies are filled with treasures — just like the Cave of Wonders. Mix together: 1 cup margarine, 1 cup brown sugar, 1 cup sugar, 2 eggs, 1 teaspoon vanilla. Add 2-1/2 cups flour, 1 teaspoon baking soda, 1 teaspoon baking powder, 2-1/2 cups oatmeal, 1 cup of either yogurt raisins, chocolate chips, or nuts. Drop in small nugget shapes on a cookie sheet. Bake at 350 degrees for 10 minutes. Let cool and enjoy.

Create a Magic Copter

Aladdin may travel on a magic carpet, but your child can make her very own toy helicopter. You'll need to help make the first helicopter, but once she gets the hang of it, your child will be able to build a fleet. You'll need paper, child-safe scissors, a ruler, pencil, paper clip, and crayons. Cut a rectangle 8-1/2 inches by 3 inches. Cut again as shown, then fold in the bottom flaps. Fold the top flaps in opposite directions. Attach a paper clip to the bottom. Your child can use crayons to decorate. Drop the helicopter and watch it spin to the ground.

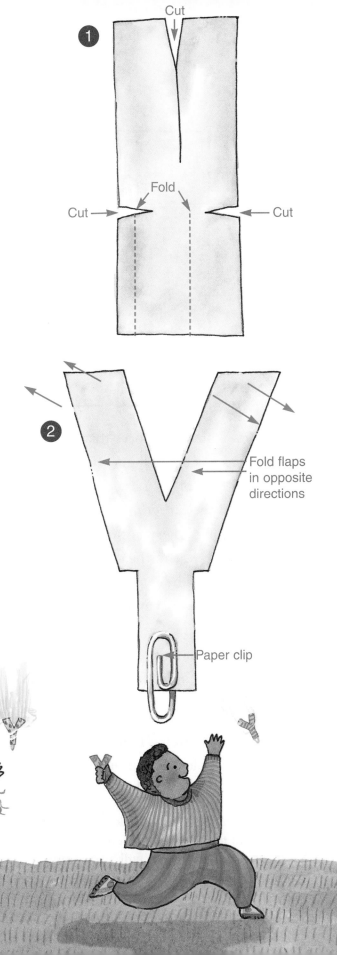

Disney's
Beauty the *BEAST*

THE PERFECT PARTY

And that's just what they did. They minded their manners. They sipped their drinks politely. They were careful not to spill a drop or smudge.

They always said please and thank you. In fact, that's about all they said, because they were trying so hard to be perfect.

Mrs. Potts announces that she will throw the most wonderful party ever. The castle's inhabitants offer to help. But all their efforts end in disaster. Finally a harried Mrs. Potts shoos everyone out of her kitchen and sets to work herself. Fearing a repeat of the earlier mishaps, the guests remain on their best behavior during the party, making it very boring and dreary. But when Belle accidentally dumps the party cake on Cogsworth's head, Mrs. Potts laughs and everyone relaxes and begins to have fun. The party ends up a grand success. This book helps children learn that:

- friends try to help one another.
- enjoying the unexpected makes life fun.
- making mistakes is a natural part of life.
- good friends can make any occasion enjoyable.

Put On Your Thinking Cap

Small children love parties and will easily identify with the adventures of Mrs. Potts and her friends. Read this story to your child. Afterwards, your child will probably be able to tell what happened in his own words. Gentle prompts will allow your child to share what he remembers. Here are a few examples:

- Why did Mrs. Potts want to have a party?
- Why do you think Mrs. Potts sent Cogsworth out of her kitchen?

- Mrs. Potts asked everyone to leave her kitchen. Why?
- How did her guests act when they were trying to be perfect?
- What did Mrs. Potts learn from this party?

One level of comprehension is understanding what is behind the actions of the characters in the story. Here are some simple "why" questions that can help your child with this skill. Remember, with very small children, there are no wrong answers. All responses should be encouraged.

- Why did Lumiere tiptoe out of the kitchen?
- Why did Mrs. Potts ask Belle to take Chip and Footstool out to play?
- Why was Mrs. Potts so tired and cranky by the end of the day?

Party Time

No excuse is needed to throw a party! Your child can have a terrific time putting on a party for a group no larger than himself and you (and perhaps a few stuffed animals). But whatever the number of party-goers, a party can make any day more fun. Your child can start by making invitations. Any sheet of paper can be folded in half and colored. Under your supervision, paste or glue stick can be used to add bits of colored tissue paper, yarn, and foil to brighten up the invitation(s).

Candies Count

Of course, just as in Mrs. Potts's party, fun foods make a party special. Something as simple as colored candies can make for a party atmosphere — and good math. For small children, gummy-type or coated chocolate candies work best. Here are some ways to help your child practice a number of math skills:

- Have your child sort a packet of colored candies into groups of the same color.
- Have your child explore simple math by counting up the number of candies in each pile.
- Have your child decide which pile has the most, and which has the least, candies.
- Ask your child if there are patterns that can be made with the candies. For example: two orange candies, three blue candies, two orange candies. What comes next?

Let Them Eat Cake

What party is complete without a cake? Use cake mix to make two layers in nine-inch round pans. Let your child help measure and mix. When the layers have cooled, set one aside. From the other, cut out ear shapes. Now position the ears above the other layer to make a bunny. Purchase or make frosting and let your child frost the cake. After the frosting is on, add licorice strips for whiskers and gum drops or raisins for eyes.

Or your child may decide to make a cake of his own design. Once again, use a cake mix. Purchase or make frosting and let your child use his imagination to decorate the cake. Some items to have available include: food coloring, gumdrops, licorice, and colored candies. Be sure to take a photo of this work of art before you eat it!

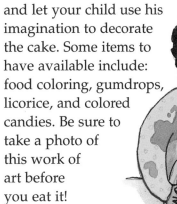

The Seven Dwarfs had an unexpected guest. She was the beautiful, kindhearted princess Snow White — and she had chosen their very own cozy cottage for her home. To show them how much she appreciated staying with them, Snow White had cleaned their cottage from top to bottom and cooked them a delicious soup for their dinner.

That night, as they danced and sang along with their new friend, the dwarfs thought how much merrier Snow White made everything seem.

The Seven Dwarfs agree to do something nice for Snow White while she sleeps late. They try to clean up, make muffins, and gather flowers for the Princess. But they end up making a mess of things. While the dwarfs are out of the house, Snow White sets everything right. The dwarfs, unaware of Snow White's help, proudly treat her to breakfast. Though she did most of the work, the Princess is happy because she learns how much her new friends care for her. This story teaches children that:

- ❂ friends enjoy doing nice things for one another.
- ❂ it's the thought that counts, not the gift.
- ❂ when everyone shares the load, work can be fun.

Put On Your Thinking Cap

Who, what, when, where, why? These are the basic questions not only of journalists, but of good readers. Children are reading with good comprehension if they can go back over a story and answer the "Five Ws." Practice with your child by asking questions like these:

- Who is staying at the house of the Seven Dwarfs?
- What meal do the dwarfs agree to make for Snow White?
- When should the berries for Dopey's muffins have been picked?

- Where do Happy and Bashful go to pick flowers?
- Why does Snow White enjoy the special breakfast so much, even though she did most of the work?

This story is filled with gentle humor as one snafu after another messes up the dwarfs' efforts. You can help your child follow the mix-ups by asking her about each of the dwarfs:

- What did Sleepy do when he tried to sort out the silverware?
- What happened when Dopey tried to make muffins?
- Why did the clothes Doc and Bashful washed become muddy?
- Why did Happy and Sneezy take so long to gather flowers?
- What song did Grumpy invent?

Ice Cream Muffins

Help your child make these light and fluffy treats, then sit down and have a meal like the one Snow White shared with the dwarfs. These muffins are easy to make, and the recipe can serve as a great introduction to simple measuring skills. The ingredients are simple:

- 2 cups softened vanilla ice cream
- 1 egg
- 2 tablespoons vegetable oil
- 2 cups self-rising flour

Combine the ice cream, egg, and oil in a bowl. Mix in the flour. Fill muffin cups 2/3 full. Bake the muffins at 425 degrees for 20 to 25 minutes. Let them cool and eat up!

Flowers for a Princess

Sneezy and Happy wanted to give Snow White flowers. Your child can make some flowers to give away, too. Help her cut flower shapes out of colored paper. Paste them onto heavy green paper cut in the shapes of stems. Pick leaves from the garden and staple or paste them onto the stems as well. Have your child arrange them in a bouquet or as a centerpiece for the dinner table.

Tongue Twisters

Like all of us, Doc sometimes has trouble wrapping his tongue around certain words. Children can get great pleasure from deliberately trying to tie up their tongues. Share a giggle with your youngster by saying this tongue twister together:

Swan swam over the sea.
Swim, swan, swim;
Swan swam back again.
Well swum, swan.

Volume
6

WALT DISNEY'S
THE
JUNGLE
BOOK

A FRIEND FOR LIFE

By the time Sheba awoke, Baloo and Bagheera had decided the cubs couldn't possibly return to the jungle with an injured mother. And by the next day, they realized that not all tigers were like Shere Khan. They happily took care of the noble tigress and her family until she was strong again.

As she prepared to leave, Sheba said gratefully, "Thank you for your kindness. If there is anything I can ever do for you, please send word and I promise I will come."

Because lending a hand is what good neighbors — be they tigers, bears, panthers, or Man-cubs — do.

Mowgli leaves the Man-village to visit his friends in the jungle. On the way, he meets an injured tigress. She tries to scare Mowgli away from her cubs, but the curious lad is soon playing with the baby tigers. Mowgli and the tigress are both surprised to find themselves forming a friendship of sorts. Mowgli convinces the tigress to seek help and takes her to meet his old pals Baloo and Bagheera. At first they are very worried, but soon they learn that, unlike Shere Khan, this tigress is not a man-eater. Like the jungle's inhabitants, your child will learn that:

- good neighbors help one another.
- it is important to judge each creature for who it is.
- even the strongest creatures need help now and then.

Put On Your Thinking Cap

Expand your child's enjoyment of the story by asking the following questions:

- How did the tigress hurt herself? Discuss with your child how to stay safe while playing.
- What really brave thing did Mowgli do when he saw the tigress? Ask your child to act like an angry tigress, roaring and bounding through the jungle. You can play the part of Mowgli.
- What does your child think would have happened to the cubs if Mowgli hadn't offered to help?
- Does your child think Baloo and Bagheera were right to be concerned about the tigress?

Bye-Bye, Boo-Boos!

Just as Mowgli helps the tigress, your child might one day be called on to help others. This story is a great jumping-off point for teaching very simple first aid. With the help of one of your child's stuffed animals, dolls, or large action figures, you can demonstrate some simple techniques. While these won't qualify your child as a paramedic, he will enjoy that favorite childhood game, pretending to be a doctor. Start with a cloth, a roll of gauze, and some tape. Can your child make a simple arm sling for his stuffed animal? How about a leg splint? (Add a drinking straw to use as a splint for this one.) No gauze? Cut a rag into long strips — even toilet paper can work! Or you can always dig up your child's toy doctor kit and let his imagination run wild.

Hide and Seek

A tigress's stripes work perfectly to camouflage her in the shadows of the jungle. Your child can learn how camouflage works by playing the following game. Take three colored pipe cleaners. Help your child twist two of the pipe cleaners around the third, and bend them into an insect shape. Then you can hide the "insect" somewhere in your back yard or home. Keep it uncovered, in plain sight. When is it hardest to find? When it is put among a lot of other colors? When it is lying among leaves? Try all kinds of color combinations and test your child's spotting skills.

Ants on a Log

Here's a simple "jungle" snack your child can make himself. You will need celery, cream cheese or peanut butter, and raisins. Wash and cut celery stalks in half. Give your child a plastic knife and let him spread peanut butter or cream cheese inside the celery. Top with ants (raisins). Enjoy this tasty and healthy snack.

Creatures Beware

Mowgli proved he was a good friend to the tigress by protecting her cubs. Your child can pretend to scare away frightening creatures with this simple noisemaker. You will need two paper cups, masking tape, beans, and foil. Fill one cup with beans. Turn the other cup upside down and put it on top of the first cup. Tape the two cups together. Cover with foil, and your noisemaker is done. This tool is also useful for scaring away monsters or other unwanted nighttime creatures.

"You said 'most,'" the Little Mermaid continued, her spirits rising. "What happened to the others?"

"Funny you should ask," Mariner said with a twinkle in his eye. He reached under the table and brought out an elaborately carved coral box.

The Little Mermaid's sisters got up from their chairs and crowded in closer. Now they were almost as curious as Ariel.

King Triton throws a banquet for his neighbor, King Mariner. Sebastian the crab is put in charge of teaching Triton's daughters how to behave properly at the big event. But the youngest mermaid, Ariel, is sure that the party will be a big bore. Then, on the big night, Ariel is fascinated when the visiting king tells stories about shipwrecks and finding human possessions. King Mariner gives Ariel a ruby necklace found in a sunken pirate ship. Instead of being bored by the party, Ariel has a great time. This story teaches that:

🔹 young and old often have more in common than they think.

🔹 age is not a barrier when two people share a common interest.

🔹 preconceptions are often wrong.

Put On Your Thinking Cap

A more advanced comprehension skill involves applying what has been learned to new situations. Examples of questions that would strengthen such application skills include:

• What would you do if you could be a mermaid or merman for a day?

• If King Mariner came to dinner at your house, what would you talk about?

• If you were Sebastian, how would you show your mom or dad how to correctly hold a spoon?

In this story, Ariel discovers that she enjoys the company of an older person. What older people does your child deal with?

Are there grandparents or neighbors with whom your child comes into contact? Does your child see any similarities between the people she knows and the characters in the story? You might ask your child:

- If Grandfather were in the story, who would he be?
- If Auntie came to Ariel's feast, what would she wear, where would she sit, and what do you think she'd talk about?
- Who does King Triton remind you of?

One of the best ways for a child to show appreciation of an older relative is by writing a letter or drawing a picture. Below are some activities designed to help your child with letters of every kind.

The Write Stuff

With the story fresh in your child's mind, there's no better time for her to write a card or draw a picture to send to a relative. A simple crayon drawing will make both the sender and receiver happy. It is easy for your child to make her own writing kit.

She will need an empty coffee can with a transparent plastic lid. Make sure there are no sharp edges on the can. Next, help your child decorate the outside of the can by gluing on old wrapping paper, buttons, comic pages from the newspaper, or fabric swatches. Put a pencil, crayons, paper, a watercolor pen, a small sponge, and child-safe scissors into the can. Whenever your child wants to write or draw, she has her own special place to keep her tools.

To use the can in a learn-my-letters game, do the following. Have your child use the lid of the can to trace circles on paper. Now cut the circles out. In clear, bold printing, write a capital letter and a small letter on

each circle. Your child can practice writing the alphabet by putting the see-through lid over a letter circle, then using the watercolor pen to trace the letters onto the lid. Show your child how to wipe the lid clean with the damp sponge, and she is ready to try another letter circle.

Love Grows

Why not give an older relative a "living" letter? You will need to buy some mixed birdseed and a small bag of potting soil, or simply take some soil from your garden. Cut a cardboard milk carton in half the long way. Have your child fill one of the milk carton pieces halfway up with potting soil. Lightly water the soil. Now have your child trace "I ♥ YOU" about 1/2 inch deep in the soil. If she needs help, you can guide your child's finger. Have your child thickly sprinkle the bird seed into the small depressions made by the tracing. Lightly cover the seeds with soil and mist them daily or water them slightly. In eight to ten days, your child's love letter will be written in thick wild grasses, ready to give to someone special.

"You know," said the Fairy Godmother, "I might have let you use the wand if only you had asked permission."

Jaq brightened. "Permission? Really? How 'bout we try one more time? We could fix things."

"What's the magic word?" asked the Fairy Godmother.

"Bibbidi-bobbidi-boo!" said Jaq.

"Not this time," she replied. "Guess again."

Gus hopped up and down. "Zuk-zuk!" he cried.

"Magic word . . . please!"

It is the morning after the big ball, and Cinderella's two mouse friends, Jaq and Gus, find something sparkly. It is the Fairy Godmother's magic wand. Without asking permission, the two play with it and find themselves magically changed into horses, then bees, and finally dogs. With every change the pair turn the household ever more topsy-turvy, and poor Cinderella despairs as she looks over the wreckage. The Fairy Godmother returns, and the sorry mice ask permission to use the wand one last time. They use it to bring order back to the household. Children learn from this story that:

- "please" is the most magical word of all.
- you should always ask permission before playing with someone else's things.
- it isn't fair to make a mess while playing and then let someone else do all the cleanup.
- when you cause a problem, you should apologize and help make things right.

Put On Your Thinking Cap

It's fun to imagine yourself as a different creature. What animal would your child wish to become? Why? Discuss how the creatures Jaq and Gus turned into are different from mice. Use these questions as a help:

- When they became horses, what did Jaq and Gus do?
- What did Jaq do first when he became a bee?
- How did the two get back at Lucifer the

cat for all the times he chased them as mice?

- Would you chase the mean stepsisters if you became a bee? Why?

Analyzing the pictures in a story is an important comprehension skill. You can choose a picture in the story and ask your child questions like:

- What do you think is happening in the picture?
- What do you think will happen next?

A fun memory game is to allow your child to carefully examine a picture, then hide it and ask questions such as:

- What colors were the horses Gus and Jaq turned into?
- What color was the handle of Cinderella's broom?

It's in the Bag!

Children love to fingerpaint, but it can often make a big mess. Here's a fingerpainting recipe that's fun, easy, and mess-free. Put 1/4 cup liquid detergent and 3 tablespoons tempera paint into a large, see-through plastic bag with "zipper" closure. Seal tightly. Lay the bag on a flat surface and let your child finger paint. He can make beautiful pictures over and over, with no cleanup required.

Mother, May I?

Here is a classic childhood game that emphasizes the importance of good manners, one of the lessons Jaq and Gus learn in the story. In Mother (Father), May I? the players stand at one end of the room or lawn and ask "Mother, may I take three baby steps?" The person who is *It* stands at the other side of the room and says "Yes, you may" or "No, you may not."

The players gradually narrow the space between themselves and Mother. The first person to reach Mother becomes *It*. Players can vary their requests with fun steps like hops, giant steps, skips, scissor steps, and the like.

Animal Crackers

Here's a tasty way to practice sorting and coordination skills. Your child will need a box of animal crackers, paper, child-safe scissors, pencil, paste, clothespins, and margarine tubs. Take one of each shape cracker from the box and trace it on the paper. Cut out the tracings and paste each one on a separate clothespin. Snap each clothespin onto the edge of a margarine tub. Now your child can sort the rest of the real animal crackers into the correct tubs. And, of course, eat a few.

Walt Disney's
DUMBO

NOT SO FAST!

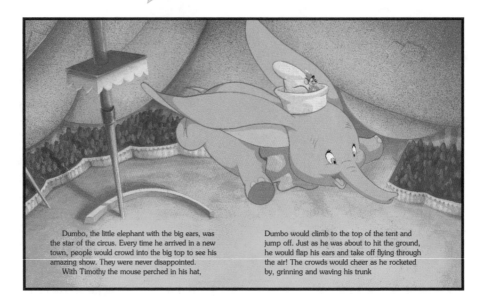

Dumbo, the little elephant with the big ears, was the star of the circus. Every time he arrived in a new town, people would crowd into the big top to see his amazing show. They were never disappointed. With Timothy the mouse perched in his hat,

Dumbo would climb to the top of the tent and jump off. Just as he was about to hit the ground, he would flap his ears and take off flying through the air! The crowds would cheer as he rocketed by, grinning and waving his trunk

Dumbo loves speed. The slow, methodical ways of the other elephants make him impatient. Dumbo flies through his tasks so quickly, however, that he doesn't always do a good job. When Dumbo decides to surprise the other elephants and set up the Big Top all by himself, he skips crucial steps. The result is so shoddy that a wind lifts the circus tent off its poles. The elephants work together to repair the damage, and their careful teamwork soon sets everything right. Dumbo learns some lessons, and so do children reading this story:

- anything worth doing is a thing worth doing well.
- speed can be fun, but slowing down allows you to be more thorough.
- teamwork makes a job go faster.
- you can be proud of a job well done.

Put On Your Thinking Cap

Applying what has been learned from a story to a situation in the real world requires a higher level of understanding. A first step in strengthening this comprehension skill is to make sure your child does indeed understand what she has been reading. A few simple questions can help set the stage for these application skills:

- Why did Dumbo fly ahead of the train?
- What was the problem with the way Dumbo did his chores?
- What lesson did Dumbo learn?

Now your child may be ready to apply what she has learned about Dumbo and his friends in this story to other situations. Your child can have some fun acting out these scenarios:

- Imagine that Dumbo is cleaning your room. How do you think he'd do the job?
- Pretend you are Timothy waking from sleep high up in the air.
- Use a stuffed animal and show how Mrs. Jumbo might scold Dumbo.

Bubble Fun

Dumbo soars high in the air, and so can bubbles of all shapes and sizes. Use this recipe to make your own bubble solution: 1/4 cup liquid detergent, 3/4 cup water, and 4 drops glycerin (available at a pharmacy). Help your child make a variety of wands. She can bend pipe cleaners into different shapes, tape several straws together, cut the bottom out of a paper cup or use a piece of string with the ends tied together. Let her experiment to see which wands make the biggest bubbles, the smallest, the most unusual bubbles, etc.

Paper Parachutes

For more flying fun, try this experiment. You will need string, tape, paper, and a small plastic object. Cut a seven-inch square of paper. Tape string to each corner of the square and tie the other ends of the string to a plastic figure as shown. Drop the parachute yourself, or make sure you supervise your child as she

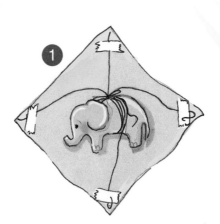

stands on a small chair and drops the parachute. Now make the string longer. Then try a heavier object. How about a round parachute? Which gives the fastest rides, the best landing? Which kind of parachute would she rather use?

The Big Top

Children can make instant "Big Top" tents by draping an old sheet over the back of the sofa and a chair or two. A few favorite toys dragged inside, along with an apple, a flashlight, and Disney's Storytime Treasures Library books, and your child can happily play and read in her own private world.

Tell a Tale

Children love to read their own stories. Even young children with no writing skills can dictate a short, simple story that an adult can write down for them. Have your child make up a new story about Dumbo's adventures. As she tells it to you, print a sentence or two at the bottom of blank sheets of paper. Your child can then illustrate these pages using crayons or child-safe markers. Staple the resulting pages together and — presto! — your child has become an author. Now read the book aloud to your child.

Disney's
POCAHONTAS
AN UNLIKELY PAIR

From that day on, Meeko looked forward to spending time together with Percy. The strange visitor from another land had become his trusted friend. And while it was true that Meeko had taught an old dog some new tricks, that little raccoon had learned a few things himself.

The spoiled dog Percy doesn't know how to act in Pocahontas's village. His inconsiderate behavior annoys the residents, and Percy is sent away to the wilds. Percy can only survive by following Meeko the raccoon, and copying all his actions. At first Meeko doesn't think very highly of Percy, but gradually the two become friends. When a mother bear threatens the pair, Percy risks his life to save Meeko. Pocahontas tells the villagers of Percy's heroism. The Indians honor Percy by making him a member of the tribe. Children learn from this tale that:

- you won't win friends with selfish behavior.
- you can learn new things by watching others closely.
- love and trust bring out the best in all creatures.
- brave and selfless actions are greatly admired.

Put On Your Thinking Cap

Children enjoy looking at the smallest details of a story. Here are a few questions to encourage that comprehension skill:

- What are three things that raccoons eat?
- What are two things in the story that happen indoors?
- Can you name three characters whose names begin with a "p" sound?
- What is one thing in the story that could not have happened in real life?

Ready for Action

You don't have to be lost in the woods like Percy to face hurdles that have to be overcome. All children love obstacle courses and physical challenges. Here are a few you can try in your own home. Besides having fun, your child will be developing his coordination and muscles.

Paper Bag Jump
How many times can your child jump over a large open paper bag in fifteen seconds? Thirty seconds? One minute? Have him try jumping sideways, then back and forth.

Card Flip
Put a small wastebasket in the center of the room. Using a deck of cards, how many cards can your child flip into the trash can? While sitting down?

Coin Balance
Put three pennies in a stack on your child's elbow while it is folded in front of him. Can he walk around the room without spilling the coins?

Limbo
Hold up a yardstick waist high. Can your child limbo underneath? How low can he go?

Cross the River
Put a jump rope on the ground in a straight line. Can your child balance while walking along the rope? Try putting a few twists in it. Make the rope into a circle.

Obstacle Course
Can you construct an indoor obstacle course for your child? Ideas might include having him slide along the floor on his tummy, going over a pillow, under a kitchen chair, around a staggered set of chairs or toys, or any other imaginative use of household items.

Nature in a Bag

Take your child on a nature hike and collect leaves, seeds, twigs, and other treasures. When you return home, sort these treasures and put them into plastic bags with "zipper" closures. Have your child dictate a sentence about the contents of each bag. Write it on a piece of white tape. Place sentences onto the bags and staple the bags together to form your child's book of nature.

Disney's
HERCULES
LIGHTNING STRIKES

As they were happily swooping through the air, weaving around the clouds, they didn't notice that the sky had grown darker. Before they knew it, they were in the middle of a thunderstorm, with lightning bolts flashing all around them.

Hercules guessed that these lightning bolts were being hurled from the top of Mount Olympus by his father, Zeus. Determined to know that same feeling of power, Hercules flew after a stray lightning bolt, then reached out and caught it in his hand.

Hercules wants to be a hero and is sent to Philoctetes for training. Phil discovers that Hercules does have godlike strength, but he also acts without thinking. The result is always disastrous. When the city of Thebes faces sudden ruin from an invading army, Hercules makes the city's troubles worse with one unthinking action after another. All seems lost until Hercules has an idea that uses his brain instead of his muscle. Hercules goes to the invaders and tells them he's decided to be on their side. This idea proves so terrifying that they immediately retreat. Like Hercules, children learn from this story that:

- you should think before you act.
- strength alone is not enough to deal with difficult events.
- quick reactions aren't always the right ones.

Put On Your Thinking Cap

Hercules learns one of the universal lessons of childhood — might does not make right. Help your child appreciate this tale more fully with questions and activities like these:

- Do you know someone who reminds you of Hercules? In what way?

- When does the story take place? Look at the pictures and tell what clues you see that make it clear this story happened long ago.
- If Hercules came to visit and helped you clean up your bedroom, what might happen?

Super Strength Cookies

These cookies take lots of strength and energy to make. Put 3 cups oatmeal, 1-1/2 cups brown sugar, 1-1/2 cups flour, 1-1/2 cups margarine, and 1-1/2 teaspoons baking powder in a large bowl.

Combine ingredients and then let your child mash the dough, knead it, and pound it. The harder and longer she mixes it, the better it will taste. Roll dough into small balls and place on a cookie sheet. Bake at 350 degrees for 10 minutes. Be sure to let cool before eating.

Stronger Than Hercules

Here are some fun activities to build strong muscles.

FOR ARM STRENGTH

Crab Walk — Have your child sit on the floor, lift her bottom, and move about the room on hands and feet.

Wheelbarrow — For this exercise, your child lies face down on the floor. Grasp her legs, and ask her to extend her arms forward and "walk" on her hands.

Push Down a Wall — Ask you child to push the palms of her hands against a wall, hard, for fifteen seconds. Now have her try it with fingertips only.

Knees Up — Help your child do a push-up with knees on the ground. This is a real challenge for young bodies.

FOR LEG STRENGTH

Paper Bag Jump — In this exercise, your child stands beside a large paper bag. She jumps sideways over it, then back again.

Squat Jump — Ask your child to clasp her hands behind her head and squat. Now ask her to jump up.

Standing Broad Jump — For this one, your child jumps as far forward as possible. First she should start with arms down and back. Then she can swing them forward and up with the jump for extra spring.

After a few hours they stopped to take a break. When they did, Thumper hopped onto a log and began thumping it with his foot.

"It sounds good," said Thumper, "but I think something's missing."

He smiled at Edgar, who jumped up beside him and pounded the log with his tail. A loud thumping echoed through the forest. Thumper joined in, and soon the woods were filled with a happy rhythm, a neighborly beat that was part thump and part thud — part welcome and part thank-you.

Edgar Beaver is the new neighbor in the woods. He immediately gets busy building a house and a dam. The problem is, it's located in the stream right below Thumper's house. Not only is the beaver causing all kinds of noise and commotion, he even has the nerve to thump on Thumper's favorite log. Then one night, heavy rains swell the beaver pond and threaten Thumper's home. Edgar destroys his own home in order to save Thumper's. After this, Edgar and Thumper each apologize and the two work together to rebuild Edgar's house. This story teaches children that:

- good neighbors welcome newcomers to the neighborhood.
- neighbors should be thoughtful and respect each other.
- neighbors can work together to overcome disaster.

Put On Your Thinking Cap

Applying what's been learned in a story to another situation is a key comprehension skill. Try some of these ideas to extend your child's understanding:

- Invite your child to act out Edgar's rescue of Bambi, using favorite stuffed animal toys.

- Have your child pretend he is Thumper and ask him if he can make music using his body.
- Have any new neighbors moved in? How does your child think they feel about their new neighborhood? Or have you recently moved? Use the story as a jumping-off point for a discussion.

- Has your child made any new friends recently? Is the new friend most like Bambi or Thumper, Flower or Edgar? Why?
- Thumper has a favorite log. What is your child's favorite play place? Have him show you.

The Sounds of Music

Thumper is not the only one who can make music. While Thumper uses a hollow log, your child can make drums from empty coffee cans and clean, empty tin cans (just make sure there are no sharp edges) or overturned kitchen pots. Different sizes produce different pitches. Wooden rulers or even old wooden spoons make good drumsticks.

Another simple musical instrument can be made by stretching different-sized rubber bands around a strong shoe box with the lid off. Pluck the rubber bands and presto! Your child has a banjo.

Filling a few soda bottles with water can produce a sound similar to a panpipe. Just make sure that each bottle has a different amount of water in it. Then set them on a tabletop that's a convenient height for your child. When he blows across the top of each bottle, a note is produced. By blowing across first one bottle, then another, a regular symphony of notes can be made.

Water, Water Everywhere

The rushing water was frightening to Edgar and Thumper, but water can be fun, too. Fill a sink or dishpan with some water. Gather some small household objects for this experiment. Have your child make predictions about what will float and what will sink. Some items to try: soap, corks, sponges, spoons, a bottle with a cap on, a bottle without the cap, small plastic toys.

When you have finished this activity, use the remaining water in the tub to let your child "paint." Give your child a large paintbrush or paint roller and allow him to paint the outside of your home with water. Be sure to admire his handiwork.

Volume
13

Walt Disney's
Pinocchio
NOSE FOR TROUBLE

everyone if they'd seen the cuckoo. He climbed the bell tower, peering out across the sky. Next he bought a birdhouse and some seeds, hoping the cuckoo would stop by for a snack.

Wherever Pinocchio went, Jiminy Cricket followed along behind, trying to talk to him. But Pinocchio wouldn't listen to his conscience.

Geppetto, the master toy maker, is creating a cuckoo clock using a caged cuckoo as his model. Despite warnings to leave the bird alone, Pinocchio opens the birdcage, and the cuckoo flies away. Pinocchio fibs to his father about what happened and blames Figaro, the cat. Pinocchio's nose begins to grow and continues to grow as one lie leads to another. Before long, Pinocchio's nose is the size of a broomstick. Finally Pinocchio tells the truth and apologizes for lying. Immediately, his nose shrinks back to normal. In reading this story, children will learn that:

- ❂ telling the truth is always the right thing to do.
- ❂ one lie leads to another.
- ❂ if you are genuinely sorry, people who love you will forgive your mistakes.

Put On Your Thinking Cap

Going through this book with your child can provide a springboard for an exploration of right and wrong. Here are a few simple questions and games to get the discussion going:

- What do you think Geppetto would have said if Pinocchio had admitted right away that he had opened the birdcage?
- How do you think you would feel after telling all those lies? Do you think you would be able to finally tell the truth?
- Pretend you are Pinocchio, and give Jiminy Cricket some good reasons why you are eating a big cookie right before

dinner — even though Geppetto told you not to. Now pretend you are Jiminy and tell Pinocchio what you think of his reasons.

Clay Play

Your child can sculpt and create just like Geppetto in his workshop. Make up a batch of salt clay and then let your tiny sculptor go to work. Mix 1 cup flour and 1 cup salt. Add just enough water for the mixture to feel like modeling clay. It should not be too sticky or too dry. To add color, put a few drops of food coloring in the water before mixing. Or paint the completed project with poster paints before popping it in a 200-degree oven. Most projects will need to be in the oven for about 5 minutes. Thicker projects can take up to an hour to harden. Store leftover clay in a tightly sealed plastic bag.

Salt clay sculptures can be fashioned into any shape your child can imagine. Rolling pins can be used to flatten the dough, and cookie cutters make great shapes. Beads can be made by rolling balls and poking a pencil through to make a hole for a string.

Figaro Figures

To make a cat, roll a thick ball of clay for the body and a smaller ball for the head. Pinch out ears, use a pencil to push in some eyes, and roll a fat worm-shaped piece of clay for the tail. Draw the face with a felt-tip pen, paint, and bake. To help the sculpture remain stable and solid, place the cat on a flatter piece of clay and paint it to look like a mat.

Pinocchio Pals

Help your child make a clay Pinocchio by rolling a thick ball for the body. Two thin worm shapes can be attached for arms and two for legs. Two round balls make the feet. Two smaller round balls make the hands. Add a round ball for the head, and a long, thin shape of clay for Pinocchio's nose. Then have your child paint it to look like a wooden boy.

Searching for Sounds

Pinocchio searched for the cuckoo bird. Have your child search for words beginning with "c" as in "cuckoo." Ask her to walk through the house or yard and count the number of objects she finds. Next, have her choose a letter and it's your turn to search. Continue taking turns and hunting for alphabet objects as long as your child remains enthusiastic.

Walt Disney's
Sleeping Beauty

A MAGIC PLAN

It was just then that Princess Aurora appeared carrying a bouquet of weeds. "I found these in the garden," she said. "What are they for?" Then she caught sight of the wedding gown. "And what happened to that dress?" she wondered.

Suddenly a loud CRASH was heard in another part of the castle. Moments later, the royal baker rushed in. "It's the cake!" he cried in alarm. "It's still growing — and it just broke through the roof!"

Aurora's wedding to Prince Phillip is about to take place, and the three good fairies, Flora, Fauna, and Merryweather, want to help out. Each fairy has ideas about the wedding preparations but, unfortunately, they cannot agree and so they put off making any decisions. Suddenly it is the day before the wedding and nothing is ready. Using their magic wands, the fairies go to work dreaming up the perfect wedding, but when their magic backfires, there is only one thing they can do. Setting the clocks back, they put everyone in the kingdom to sleep. Then they take the time they need to plan carefully. This story teaches young ones that:

- everyone's opinion is important.
- working together gets things done.
- careful planning pays off.

Put On Your Thinking Cap

Children with brothers and sisters won't have too much trouble identifying with the three fairies. How many times have arguments broken out in your own home about the best way to do things? Here are a few questions and activities designed to get

your child thinking about the meaning of the story:

- Are there times when you don't agree with your friends or brothers and sisters? Describe how you handled one of those times.
- Would you like to have a magic wand of

your own? What would you use it to do? Clean your room? Make cookies?

• What would you say to the three fairies if you were Aurora? What would your mom or dad say to the three fairies?

Let the Games Begin

There's nothing like a good game for getting children to work together — just like Flora, Fauna, and Merryweather learned to do. Help your child make a changeable game board using crayons or markers and 25 index cards. On one of the cards have your child draw a picture of a house. This is "Home," the goal of the game. On another card draw a picture of a boy or girl or dog. This is the "Start." On each of the other cards write messages like Move Ahead 1 (2 or 3) spaces or Go Back 1 (2 or 3) Spaces. Pictures of dragons or witches can represent loss of one turn. Pictures of flowers or hearts can mean take another turn.

Now place the cards in a wiggly line. The only rule of placement is that the "Start" card goes at the beginning and the "Home" card at the end. Use a die to move, and coins as markers. Have fun!

Celebrate!

Plan a simple party to celebrate Aurora's wedding to the Prince. Decorate the room with streamers or chains of colored paper rings.

Party Place Mats

Take a sponge and cut it into a heart shape. Moisten the sponge and wring out well. In a pie pan, mix 3 tablespoons tempera paint with 2 teaspoons liquid detergent. Have your child dip the sponge into the paint and sponge-paint hearts onto an 11"x 14" sheet of paper. Let dry and use as a place mat.

Celebration Cake

Follow the directions on a box of cake mix. Allow your child to measure and mix. Then make this simple frosting: Mix together 1-1/3 cups vegetable shortening, 1/2 cup milk, 2 pounds powdered sugar, 1/4 teaspoon salt, and 1/2 teaspoon vanilla extract. Beat until fluffy (about 8 minutes). Give your child a spoon and a plastic knife and let him decorate the cake. Items to use include: jelly beans, strands of licorice, gum-drops, colored candies, and food coloring.

Eggs-traordinary Flowers

Cut an egg carton into twelve sections. Poke a hole in each center. Provide colored tissue paper, glue, and pipe cleaners. Have your child glue colored paper on the egg flowers and put the pipe cleaners through as stems. Make several flowers and arrange them in a pretty bouquet.

The puppies gathered around the old bloodhound. "Really?" they asked. "Is that true, Uncle Trusty?" "Well," said Trusty, "as my grandpappy, Old Reliable, used to say. . . I don't recollect if I ever told you about Old Reliable, did I?"

As Trusty launched into a story, Lady gazed fondly at him. "Don't worry, Jock," she said. "We'll be happy to have Trusty stay with us."

Old Trusty comes to stay with Lady and Tramp for a week. At first the puppies love his stories, but they soon grow tired of the old dog's ways. When Scamp, the boldest puppy, hurts Trusty's feelings, the old bloodhound leaves the house and heads into the woods. Everyone goes looking for the missing Trusty. Scamp meets up with a fierce stray, but Trusty appears and saves the day. Scamp realizes there is more to Trusty than he thought. Young readers learn that:

- older folks have lots of stories to tell.
- wisdom can be gained from experience.
- you should always respect your elders.
- you should think about someone's feelings before you say something that might be hurtful.

Put On Your Thinking Cap

You can help make the connections between the characters in the story and your child's own experiences. Here's how:

- Ask your child if Trusty reminds her of someone. Why?
- Have your child act out how Scamp ate the birthday cake. Now ask her to act out how she thinks Trusty would eat the cake.
- Ask your child if she has a favorite story she likes hearing again and again. What is it? Have your child tell you the story.
- Did Scamp behave well or badly in this story? Why?

- If an elderly person were staying at your house and kept telling the same story over and over, ask your child what she would say to the visitor.

Spin a Tale

Children can be great storytellers, just like Trusty, with their very own Story Spinner. Here's how to make one: Start with a round cardboard pizza tray. Have your child cut out interesting pictures from an old magazine and paste them all around the tray. Make a small hole in the center of the tray. Push a brass paper fastener through the center hole and attach a large paper clip to it. This will be the spinner. Have your child spin the spinner. Whatever it lands on becomes the subject of your child's story.

Scamp's Scavenger Hunt

Scamp's woodland hunt for Trusty turned up an unexpected find. Take your child on a scavenger hunt through a local natural area. Here are several ideas for some challenging things to find:

Colors — Find things from nature that are purple, blue, green, yellow, red, orange, white, black, and brown. Which colors are the most common? Which are the hardest to find?

Shapes — Find objects that are different shapes: round, square, triangular, rectangular, and star-shaped. Which are the most common?

Smells — Look for items with different smells. What do some of the smells remind you of?

Touch — Find something smooth, something rough, and an object with rounded edges to touch.

Seeds — Try finding fuzzy seeds, prickly seeds, squishy seeds, hard seeds, and a seedpod. How many different seeds can you find?

Back home, have your child glue some of her finds onto a sturdy piece of cardboard to make a work of art.

Volume

16

Disney's
THE
HUNCHBACK
OF NOTRE DAME

THE HIDDEN HERO

Quasimodo lifted the children in his strong arms. "You'll be able to spot your folks better from up here," he told them. He began to walk slowly down the main street of the festival. Soon they reached the spot where Esmeralda and Djali had

just finished performing. Quasimodo was explaining to Esmeralda about the lost children when they heard frantic shouts.

"Stop! Kidnapper!" Monsieur and Madame Marceau shrieked as they confronted Quasimodo.

Quasimodo, the Hunchback of Notre Dame, loves his new life outside the church's bell tower. He is accepted and respected by the people of Paris. When a new family moves to town, Quasimodo makes friends with the children, but the parents are unable to see beyond his twisted form and regard him as a monster. During an annual festival, the newly arrived children become lost, and Quasimodo calms and helps them. But when the trio find the parents, the mother and father accuse Quasimodo of taking the children. Quasimodo's friends rush to his defense, and the parents realize their mistake in judging too quickly. This story helps teach that:

- ❂ you can't judge someone by looks.
- ❂ no matter what a person looks like, it is his or her actions that count.
- ❂ it is right to speak up and tell the truth.

Put On Your Thinking Cap

This story is about judging people for who they are, not how they look. Help your child look more deeply into the meaning of this tale with these simple questions and activities:

- How do the parents react when they

first meet Quasimodo? Ask your child what the parents could have said instead of turning away.
- If your child met Quasimodo in the street, what would he say?
- When the children got lost, they

huddled in a doorway and cried. Ask your child how he would handle the same situation. This is a perfect time to discuss what your child should do if he ever becomes lost.

- Just for fun, have your child name several things in the story that begin with a "p" sound (like Paris, puppets, people). Try this with other beginning sounds.

Puppet Pals

Dancing Puppets — Use an index card. Make two holes near the bottom. Make a face on one side of the card. Add yarn hair, bits of felt for eyes, and paper arms. Push fingers through the holes just past the second joint. Then make the puppet dance.

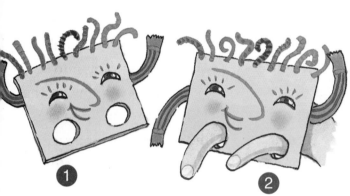

Paper Bag Puppets — Draw a face on an upside-down paper bag. Twist the corners for ears. Hold them in place with a bit of twine or a twist-tie from the supermarket. Hands go into the open side of the bag.

Funny Face Puppets — Go through old magazines and cut out eyes, noses, and mouths from the pictures found there. Paste them onto paper plates to make funny faces. Add yarn or curled strips of colored paper for hair or beards. Attach a stick or straw to the back of the paper plate as a holder.

Nature Puppets — Take a walk in your local woods or park. Gather seeds, pods, pinecones, acorns, leaves, small branches — whatever looks interesting. Make a nature puppet from these odds and ends. Start by rolling a piece of clay into a ball. Then use the "natural finds" for the features. Use grass or weeds for hair, sticks for arms, seeds for eyes.

Wind Chimes

The bells of Notre Dame have a lovely sound. Your child can make musical chimes for your home, too. Start with a paper pie plate. Turn it upside down and have an adult poke holes in it. Ask your child to find old keys, spoons, or other flat metal objects to hang from the plate. Use different lengths of yarn to tie these objects on, then place the other ends of the yarn through the holes in the plate. Knot the yarn so that it cannot slip through the holes. Hang the chimes in a windy place and listen to the melodic sounds.

"What kind of a party is this?" asked Alice.
"Why, an un-birthday party, of course," the Mad Hatter replied.
"But today *is* someone's birthday," explained Alice. "Mine!"
"Then you'll have to leave," the Mad Hatter said crossly, pointing to the window.

"But I can't fly," Alice protested.
"Time to be going!" said the White Rabbit, ignoring her. Then he took Alice's hand and pulled her out the window after him.
Outside, the White Rabbit's umbrella billowed open. As they drifted to the ground, Alice wondered, "Why didn't we just take the stairs?"

It is Alice's birthday, and she has to meet her sister at noon for a surprise. Suddenly the White Rabbit appears to warn Alice "You are late! For a very important date!" Alice follows him through one bewildering adventure after another, bumping into curious characters such as the Mad Hatter and the Queen of Hearts along the way. The journey through Wonderland ends abruptly when Alice falls to the floor and wakes up. It has all been a dream! But now she really is late for her birthday surprise. She races down to her sister and is presented with the perfect gift — an alarm clock! This story demonstrates that:

- being on time has its rewards.
- even when we are asleep, we have the ability to make up fantastic stories.

Put On Your Thinking Cap

This story is truly an unusual adventure, moving from one wacky scene to the next. You can help your child sort out and appreciate the story by going back over it and asking questions like these:

- What was your favorite adventure in the book? Why? Can you draw a picture of that scene?

- Can you act like one of the characters that Alice met? How would that character act if he or she came to dinner?

- Can you describe a strange dream you once had?

It's About Time!

Time is a difficult concept for a young child to understand. Help your child by exploring just how long a minute is. What can she do in a minute? Can she wash her hands, walk around the sofa three times, brush her hair?

Send your child on a clock hunt. Have her count how many clocks are in your house. How many are digital? How many have hands?

Following in the footsteps of the White Rabbit, your child can create her own clock. You will need child-safe scissors, a paper plate, a pencil, a piece of colored paper, and a brass paper fastener. With your help, have your child create a clock face on the paper plate, using a pencil or crayons. Then poke a hole through the center of the paper plate with the pencil point. Have your child cut out two strips from the  colored paper. Both should end in points, but one should be shorter than the other. Then simply poke the fastener through each of the two paper strips and through the hole in the center of the paper plate. Open the paper fastener out and your child has a clock that can be used for all sorts of lessons on telling time. Talk about dinnertime, bedtime, time for school, time to wake up. Show her these times on her own clock.

Seeing Red

In the story, the Queen of Hearts had a red banquet. Plan a red banquet with your child. What will you wear? What will you eat? Check your refrigerator and brainstorm some red foods: strawberries, cherries, apples, tomatoes, chips with salsa, chicken strips with ketchup, cranberry juice. Use food coloring to create red applesauce, red cottage cheese, or red eggs. Put your imagination to work to come up with some unusual red foods.

An Un-birthday Crown

Like the Mad Hatter, your child can pretend that today is her un-birthday. Make a crown from heavy paper. Have your child decorate it with gems (colored shapes of construction paper), glitter, stickers, buttons, scraps of yarn or fabric, streamers. Staple it closed, and your child's crown is ready to wear to an un-birthday celebration. Be sure to sing to the un-birthday child.

Smee led the boys inside. "What's the meaning of this, Smee?" Captain Hook demanded.

The first mate stammered, "Th-they say they were checking on your safety, sir. And I must say, they're hard workers. Just today I saw them swabbing the deck and standing lookout."

The captain looked John straight in the eye.

"Yes," he agreed, "I think they're doing a fine job. After all, with the attack only three days off, security is more important than ever."

"Attack?" said John.

Hook said, "We've discovered Peter Pan's hideout and will attack in three days." He turned to his first mate. "Release them, Smee. We've got work to do."

Peter Pan always leads the way for everyone else in Never Land. One day John decides to do things his own way, and sneaks off with his little brother Michael to spy on Captain Hook. The two boys disguise themselves as pirates and manage to fool the first mate, Mr. Smee. But the Captain recognizes the boys and tricks them into leading him to Peter Pan's hideout. Michael is captured and held on the pirate ship. He is freed only by the teamwork of everyone. Like John, children reading this story learn that:

- teamwork can often accomplish much more than a single person can.
- sometimes the best-laid plans go wrong. Friends can help deal with the problems that follow.
- when friends work together, each makes an important contribution to the total effort.

Put On Your Thinking Cap

Never Land is a magical place where anything can happen. Here are a few simple questions and activities to help your child imagine himself right there with the Lost Boys:

- What is your child's favorite place in Never Land? Why? What is his favorite place in your house? In the neighborhood? Why?
- Peter Pan and the Lost Boys meet in their special cave. Your child can draw a picture of what he thinks would be a perfect clubhouse. What special features and supplies should be included in the clubhouse?
- Something went wrong in the story.

Can your child think of another way to make it right? How would he rescue Michael?

Eye Spy

Never Land held plenty of mysteries worth spying out. So does any modern home. To construct a play magnifying glass, you will need to help your child cut out the center from a plastic lid. Leave the rim intact, as shown in the illustration. Snap a clothespin on the rim of the lid to make a handle. The result is a "magnifying glass," and though it won't actually magnify any object, it is a fun toy. Can your child look through his "magnifying glass" and find household items that are green or red? How about things that are rough or smooth? What about words with the letter "s" for spy, or household items that begin with a "p" sound — as in Peter Pan?

Look Sharp!

To pretend to see far away, your child can build a telescope like the one Captain Hook uses. The simplest way to create such a tool is to paint and decorate the cardboard tube from a roll of paper towels. Interestingly enough, when the eye is forced to focus on a narrow field of vision such as that provided by the play telescope, objects do appear sharper.

Eye Works

A pinhole camera gives a child an idea of how the eye actually works — important knowledge for budding spies. Start with an empty can. Now, using a nail and a hammer, punch a hole in the center of the can's bottom. Next, cut a piece of wax paper or tracing paper about 8 inches by 8 inches. Use the plastic rim from the magnifying glass project, or cut out the center from another lid that fits over the can snugly. Lay the wax paper on the open end of the can, and hold it in place by placing the plastic rim onto the can. Now your child can get involved in the fun. Have him cover his head with a dark towel or cloth to block out extra light. Ask him to look through the wax paper side of the can at a bright object such as a candle or lamp. The object will appear upside down. Explain to him that the human eye works the same way, receiving all images upside down. It is only in the brain that images are processed and turned right side up.

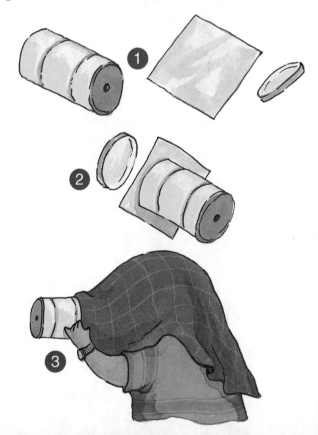